KU-021-083

Copyright © QED Publishing 2007

First published in the UK in 2007 by
QED Publishing
A Quarto Group company
226 City Road
London EC1V 2TT
www.qed-publishing.co.uk

All rights reserved. No part of this publication may
be reproduced, stored in a retrieval system, or
transmitted in any form or by any means,
electronic, mechanical, photocopying, recording,
or otherwise, without the prior permission of the
publisher, nor be otherwise circulated in any form
of binding or cover other than that in which it is
published and without a similar condition being
imposed on the subsequent purchaser.
A catalogue record for this book is available
from the British Library.

ISBN 978 1 84538 768 6

Written by Caroline Castle
Edited by Clare Weaver
Designed by Alix Wood
Illustrated by Daniel Howarth

Publisher Steve Evans
Creative Director Zeta Davies
Senior Editor Hannah Ray

Printed and bound in China

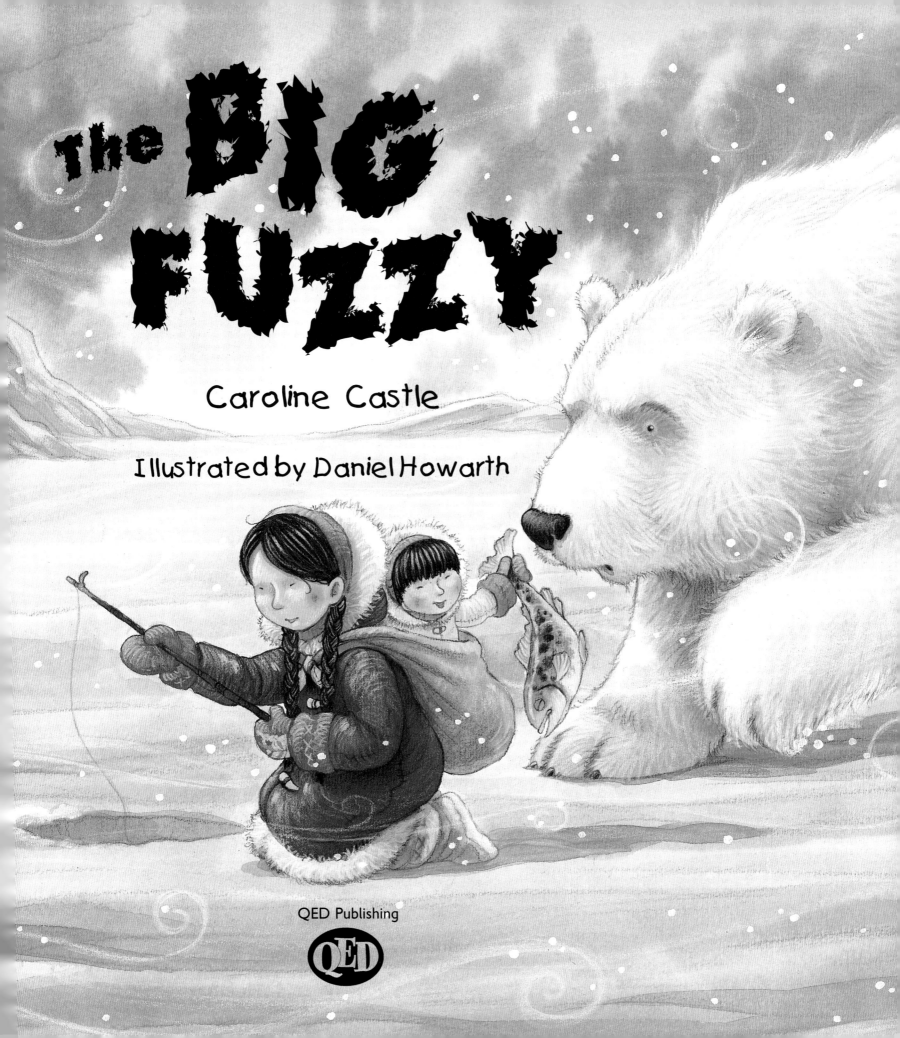

the BIG FUZZY

Caroline Castle

Illustrated by Daniel Howarth

QED Publishing

QED

This is a story that happened long ago and far away in a land covered in snow. The land was called Greenland, and still is today.

One **cold**, **cold** morning,

a domed shape rose out of the mist.

It was a little house made of ice! An **IGLOO**!

Someone was coming out of the door.
It was Little Sira, with her baby brother
Ivik strapped to her back.

Sira's mother was sick and couldn't get out of bed. Sira must go out to catch some fish for supper or the family would go hungry.

"Be safe, brave Little Sira," called her mum. "And watch out for polar bears."

But as they set off, someone saw them go. Someone **big** and **white** and **fearsome**.

Oh, it was so very cold. But Little Sira was wrapped up warm as a winter fire. She made her way slowly through the snow until she came to a good place to fish.

Little Sira dug a hole in the ice and sank her line and hook. The sun was bright in the sky, and baby Ivik was sleeping.

But someone was watching. Someone big and **white** and **fearsome**.

Very soon, Little Sira caught her first fish!

But someone big and white and **fearsome** was creeping up behind her.

Someone big and **white** and **fearsome...** and **hungry**.

Baby Ivik woke up. **"Big Fuzzy!"** he laughed at the huge, furry face.

"Here," he said, "fishy?"

The big, white creature was so surprised that he took the fish and gobbled it up.

Little Sira caught another fish, and another.

"Fishies for Fuzzy!" laughed Ivik.

The big, furry creature gobbled them all up, bones and all.

The sky grew darker.
Little Sira heard the wind howl.
It whipped up the snow
and whistled round her ears.
She knew it would soon turn into a blizzard.
It was time to pack up the fish and go home.

But when she turned round, all
the fish were gone, every one!

"Naughty Ivik!"

cried Sira.
She was very cross.

But how could her little brother have
eaten all those fish? He was much too small.
Perhaps a seal came by and took them?
Now there was nothing for the family to eat.

"Big Fuzzy,"

said Ivik.

Whoooo! Whoooo!
howled the wind.
The sky grew darker
still. Fish or no fish,
Sira knew they must
go at once, while
they could still see
the way home.

So Sira and baby
Ivik set off into the
blustery evening.
But the wind roared
like thunder and
blew snow into their
faces. Sira couldn't
see the way.

Very soon,
Little Sira
and baby
Ivik were
both lost.

The night-time fell like a thick, dark blanket.

And someone was following them. Someone **big** and white and

fearsome.

Sira saw the shadow of a huge creature behind her. "Oh, something is coming," she cried out.

"Something **huge** and **fearsome!**"

Little Sira ran as fast as she could, but the snow was thick and she was tired. Ivik felt heavy, like a big sack of potatoes tied to her back.

Soon she found herself by an icy cave. "We can hide in here," she said. They were so tired that they fell asleep straight away.

They didn't hear the big footsteps
thundering through the snow.
One, two, **three**...

Slowly, slowly, the big creature
crept inside. He opened up his
huge, strong arms, and...

...very carefully
picked up Sira and
Ivik and folded them
into his warm chest.

Then he ran and ran as fast as he could, over
the snowy hills and through the blustery blizzard,
all the way back to the igloo.

Little Sira and baby Ivik woke
up in their doorway.

Sira couldn't believe her eyes.
How did they get home?

And where did that
big fish come from?

Only baby Ivik guessed
the answer. "Big Fuzzy,"
he said happily.

Notes for Teachers and Parents

- Look at the front cover of the book together. Talk about the picture. Can the children guess what the book is going to be about? Read the title together.
- Now look at the pictures together without reading the words – what do the children think is happening?
- Read the story to the children. Build up the suspense and the excitement of what will happen next. Enjoy the rhythm of the words and the repetition of the phrase 'someone big and white and fearsome'. Were the children right when they guessed what was happening? Discuss how else the story could have ended.
- Encourage the children to take it in turns to try to read the story aloud. Help them with any difficult words and remember to praise the children for their efforts in reading the book.
- Study a map of Greenland with the children and choose a place where Sira and Ivik might live. Talk about Greenland and what life in such a cold and snowy country would be like. Here are some points to discuss: Greenland is the largest island in the world. Over 80 per cent of Greenland is covered in snow and ice. People who live there used to travel by sled. What other methods of transport might be used today to travel over the snow and ice?
- Explain to the children that Little Sira and Ivik are Inuit, which means 'the people'. In Greenland, the Inuits speak Kalaallisut, or Greenlandic. Here are some Greenlandic words that relate to the story: Kamik = boot, qanik = falling snow, panik = daughter, aqqalu = girl's younger brother, nanoq qaqortoq = polar bear, siku = ice, eqaluk = fish, puisi = seal. Make labels of the words, and encourage the children to try to say them.
- Ask the children to imagine what it would have been like to live with Sira and Ivik with no electricity, central heating or cars!
- Help the children to make a collage of a snowy landscape. Once the landscape is complete, the children can make individual drawings or paintings of the igloo and some of the the animals that might be seen in Greenland. For example; a polar bear, reindeer, seal and wolf. The drawings can then be stuck onto the collage and labelled with the names of the animals, to encourage word recognition.
- Sira and Ivik wore lots of clothes to keep themselves warm. These were made of animal skin and fur. Ask the children to think about what they would wear if they were visiting Sira and Ivik. They can draw pictures of themselves wrapped up in their warm clothes.